Clever Rabbit
and the Lion

Retold by
Susanna Davidson

Illustrated by
Daniel Howarth

Reading Consultant: Alison Kelly
Roehampton University

Once upon a time,
in a great big jungle

lived a great big lion.

ROAR!

He had great big paws
and very sharp claws.

"I'm king of the jungle," roared Lion.

"I'm going to eat you all up."

"No!" cried the jungle animals.

"You're small and weak," said Lion. "You can't stop me."

"Don't worry,"
said Clever Rabbit.
"I have a plan."

7

The next day, all the animals hid from Lion.

"Where are you all?"
roared Lion. "I want
to eat you!"

"Here I am," said
Clever Rabbit. "You
can eat me."

"I tried to come before, but a great big lion stopped me."

"I'm the only lion in the jungle," roared Lion.

"Oh no, you're not," said Clever Rabbit.

This lion has bigger paws and sharper claws!

"Show me this other lion. I'll eat him up and then I'll eat YOU."

Clever Rabbit led Lion
to the deep, wide river.

"He lives in there,"
said Clever Rabbit.

Lion looked into the water.

Another lion looked back.

Lion shook his head.

So did the other lion.

Lion leaped at the lion
in the water...

...and was swept away.

"At last," cried Clever
Rabbit. "We're safe."

The jungle animals
came rushing out.

"Help!" called Lion.
"Save me."

"We can't," said Clever
Rabbit. "We're small
and weak."

Lion let out one last
ROAR! ...

...and was never
seen again.

Puzzles

Puzzle 1

Can you spot all the animals hiding from Lion?

Can you put these pictures in order?

Puzzle 2

A   B   C   D

Puzzle 3

A   B   C   D

Puzzle 4

Spot the five differences
between these two pictures.

Answers to puzzles

Puzzle 1

lizard

snake

bird

monkey

deer

rabbit

rabbit

mouse

bugs

mouse

Puzzle 2

D   C   A   B

Puzzle 3

D   A   B   C

Puzzle 4

Series editor: Lesley Sims
Designed by Maria Pearson
and Louise Flutter

First published in 2007 by Usborne Publishing Ltd., Usborne House,
83-85 Saffron Hill, London EC1N 8RT, England. www.usborne.com
Copyright © 2007 Usborne Publishing Ltd.